INTREPID Travellers' Factopedia

Dear Reader

In 1873, a French writer named Jules Verne wrote a book called *Around the World in Eighty Days*. At that time, a journey around the world took a long time. People went by ship, train, horse and carriage, or even hot air balloon. The novel gave me the idea for this book.

Join two of the characters from Around the World in Eighty Days

... BE AN INTREPID TRAVELLER TO THE WORLD'S MOST EXTREME PLACES ...

In this book, however, I wanted to spend eighty days "travelling" to the world's most extreme places. You, too, can be an intrepid traveller – without even leaving your classroom!

I hope you enjoy your journey through this factopedia game and have some fun answering the "Intrepid Travellers' Questions" along the way!

John Parsons

NELSON
CENGAGE Learning™
For learning solutions, visit **cengage.com.au**

Contents

INTREPID TRAVELLERS' Factopedia

Tonga

Nepal

1 Prepare for the Trip

Around the **World** in Eighty Days

Phileas Fogg

In 1873, Jules Verne wrote a novel called *Around the World in Eighty Days*. It is the story of a man and his servant who travel around the world in eighty days. The man's name is Phileas Fogg. Passepartout is his servant. They travel by train and ship, and later, in the movie adaptation, they travel by hot air balloon.

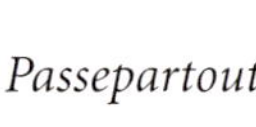

Passepartout

Eighty Days in Ten Chapters

In this book, you will "travel" for eighty days around the world in ten chapters. But there's a catch! At the end of each chapter, there's an "Intrepid Travellers' Question". You must answer it correctly before you "travel" to the next chapter.

An Extreme Challenge

If you answer the question incorrectly, "An Extreme Challenge" awaits you!

You may have to swim in an extreme place, such as Jellyfish Lake, with over ten million jellyfish. Or shiver in the world's coldest place!

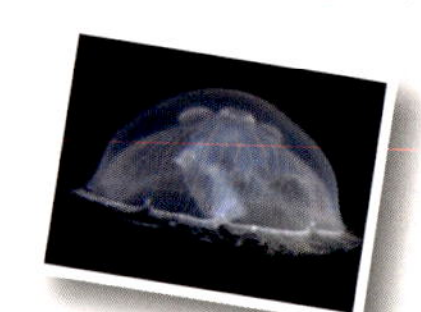

GOT YOUR PASSPORT?

Let's start at the International Date Line.

What Is the International Date Line?

The International Date Line is an imaginary line between the North Pole and the South Pole. It runs through the Bering Sea in the north, right down through the Pacific Ocean in the south.

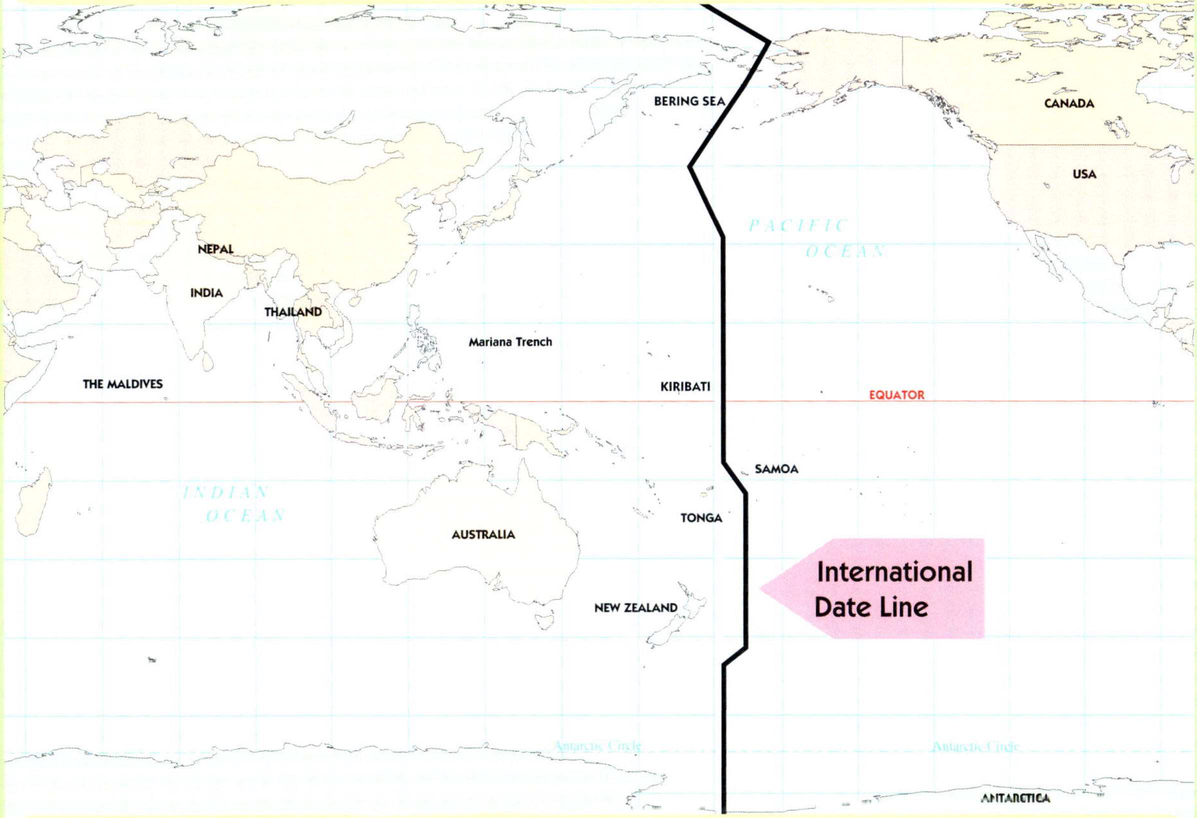

Kiribati Changed the International Date Line

The International Date Line used to run through the islands of Kiribati (pronounced "Kirribas"). This caused the islanders all sorts of problems. For example, when it was Monday in the west of Kiribati, it was still Sunday in the east. So when people in the west tried to call a shop in the east (on Monday), it would still be closed for the weekend.

So Kiribati arranged to move the date line a little eastwards. Now everyone in Kiribati is in the same day. This also means that Kiribati is the first country in the world to see the dawn of a new day!

2 From Samoa to Tonga

Days 1–5

First, all you intrepid travellers are travelling by plane from Samoa to Tonga. But before you do, read your first "Factopedia Fact" below.

Factopedia Fact

In 1892, the king of Samoa had a good idea. He wanted Samoa to be in the same day as the USA, because he thought that would help them to trade more with Samoa. But the USA was a day behind. It was on the east side of the International Date Line. Samoa was a day ahead, on the west side.

The king decided Samoa would move to the east of the date line, and Samoa is still there!

a traditional Samoan dance

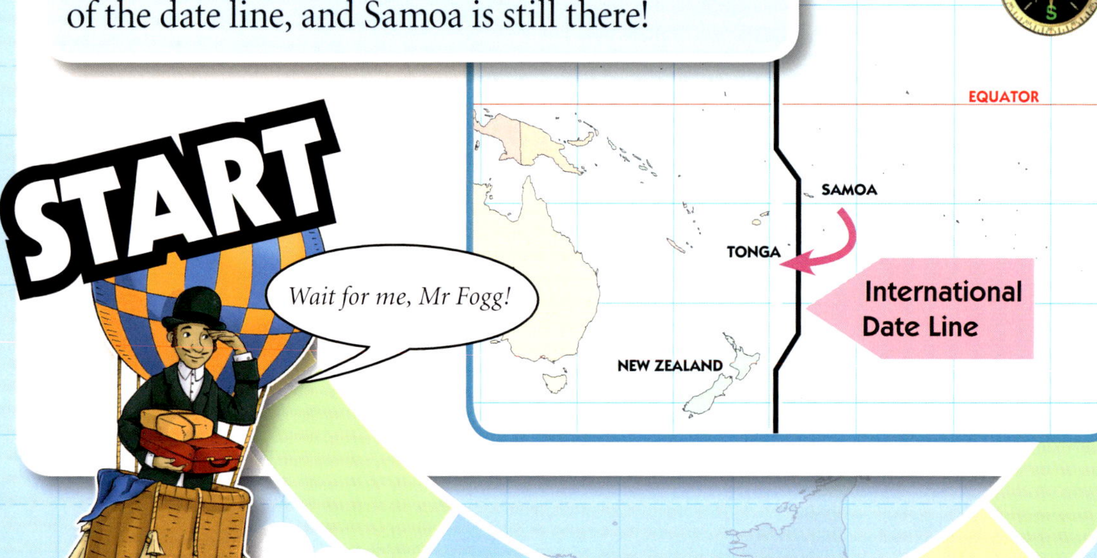

a view of the Pacific Ocean from Tonga

Intrepid Travellers' Question

You need to book a hotel room in Tonga. It takes two hours to fly from Samoa to Tonga.

If your flight from Samoa leaves on Thursday morning, what day will you check in to your Tongan room?

A. Wednesday

B. Thursday

C. Friday

If your answer was **A** or **B**, here's **AN EXTREME CHALLENGE.** We're dropping you and your surf ski off at Point Nemo. Where's that? Point Nemo is the furthest place on Earth from land. It's in the Pacific Ocean. You'll have to paddle 2688 kilometres to the nearest dry land!

(When you've finished paddling to land, hurry to page 8.)

If your answer was **C**, **YOU'RE CORRECT!** If it's Thursday in Samoa, it will be Friday in Tonga. Grab your passport. We're off to Tonga.

Go to page 8

From Tonga to the Mariana Trench

Days 6–15

After five relaxing days in Tonga, you're heading north-west by ship.

Imagine you're standing at the ship's rail speaking on your mobile phone. Suddenly you see a shark! Startled, you drop the phone and it disappears into the ocean.

Your phone has fallen into the deepest part of the Mariana Trench. It's a giant valley in the sea floor with some of the deepest water on Earth. The phone will sink an incredible eleven kilometres!

Factopedia Fact

IT'S TRUE!

In 1960, a special submarine called the *Trieste* took two explorers to a depth of 10 924 metres in the Mariana Trench. That's the deepest anyone's ever been.

the Trieste

Passepartout, I can hear the phone ringing!

a deep-sea squid

Intrepid Travellers' Question

What will happen to your phone as it falls to the deepest part of the Mariana Trench?

A. It will be eaten by a giant squid.

B. It will be crushed by the water pressure.

C. It will keep beeping until the battery runs out.

If your answer was **A** or **C**, here's **AN EXTREME CHALLENGE.** Before you continue, you must grab your bathers and go for a swim in Jellyfish Lake. This is on the Pacific island of Palau. It's only 160 metres wide and 460 metres long. Over ten million jellyfish swim in the lake!

(When you've finished swimming, hurry to page 10.)

If your answer was **B**, **YOU'RE CORRECT!** At that extreme depth, the pressure is over 1000 times greater than at the surface. The phone would be crushed. Grab your passport. We're off to Bangkok.

Go to page 10

From the Mariana Trench to Bangkok

Days 16–22

We're catching a plane for the next part of our journey. We're flying to Bangkok, the capital of Thailand.

The Thai people call their capital city Krung Thep. But its real name is longer!

a busy Bangkok river market

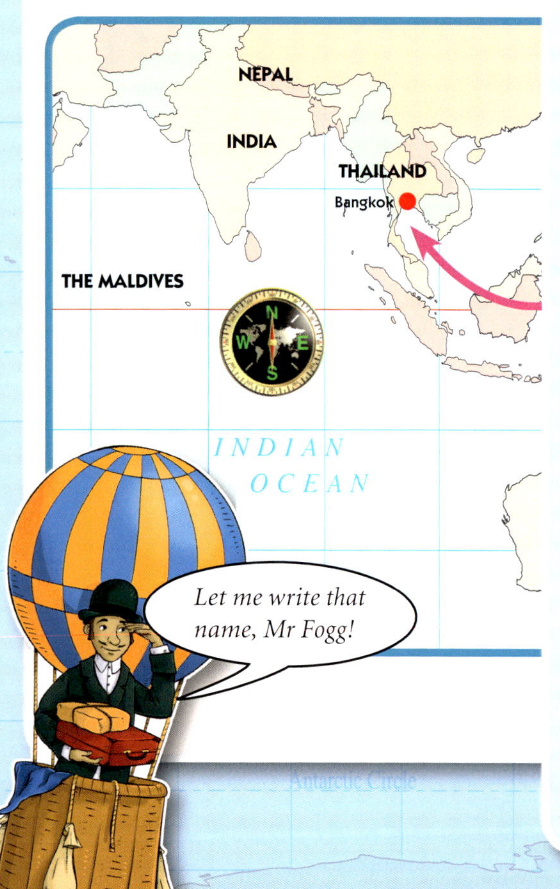

Factopedia Fact

Centuries ago, a Thai king gave Bangkok one of the longest names ever!

Imagine catching a taxi from Bangkok airport. You ask the driver to take you to central Krung Thep Mahanakhon Amon Rattanakosin Mahinthara Yuthaya Mahadilok Phop Noppharat Ratchathani Burirom Udomratchaniwet Mahasathan Amon Piman Awatan Sathit Sakkathattiya Witsanukam Prasit.

That's the *real* name for Bangkok.

Intrepid Travellers' Question

But that name isn't even the longest place name in the world. There is a hill with an even longer name. Where is the hill that has the longest name in the world?

A. Halfway between Bangkok Airport and Krung Thep Mahanakhon Amon Rattanakosin Mahinthara Yuthaya Mahadilok Phop Noppharat Ratchathani Burirom Udomratchaniwet Mahasathan Amon Piman Awatan Sathit Sakkathattiya Witsanukam Prasit

B. Between Saskatoon, Canada, and Mississippi, USA

C. In the North Island of New Zealand

Passepartout, make sure you have a long pencil!

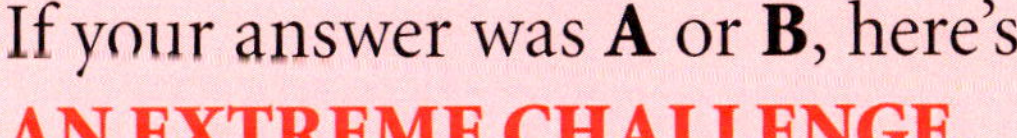

If your answer was **A** or **B**, here's **AN EXTREME CHALLENGE.** Before you continue, we're going to leave you in New Zealand. You must run up the world's steepest street. It's Baldwin Street in Dunedin. It has a steep slope of 35 degrees! Don't get too puffed!

(When you've finished running, hurry to page 12.)

If your answer was **C**, **YOU'RE CORRECT!** The name of the hill is Taumatawhakatangi-hangakoauauotamatea-turipukakapikimaunga-horonukupokaiwhenua-kitanatahu. Grab your passport. We're off to Nepal.

Go to page 12

5 From Bangkok to Nepal

Days 23–31

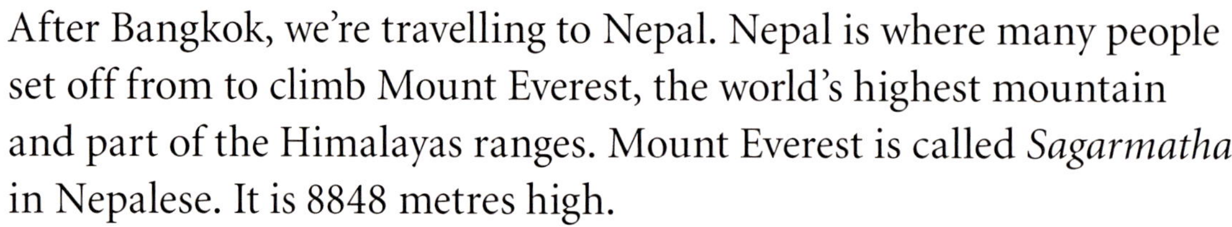

After Bangkok, we're travelling to Nepal. Nepal is where many people set off from to climb Mount Everest, the world's highest mountain and part of the Himalayas ranges. Mount Everest is called *Sagarmatha* in Nepalese. It is 8848 metres high.

Mount Everest

Factopedia Fact

What is the biggest mountain range on Earth? Some people might say the Himalayas. But the greatest mountain range is the Atlantic Ridge, under the Atlantic Ocean. It runs from Iceland almost to the Antarctic Circle. This range is over 16 000 kilometres long!

I'm sure you can manage that, Mr Fogg.

Intrepid Travellers' Question

Where is the tallest mountain when measured from its base at the bottom of the sea to its top?

A. In Hawaii

B. In Antarctica

C. In South America

lava erupts from the world's tallest mountain

If your answer was **B** or **C**, here's **AN EXTREME CHALLENGE.** Before you continue, you must spend a week on Anak Krakatau. This island was created by the eruption of the Krakatoa volcano in 1883. It was the most violent eruption in recorded history. Listen carefully for rumblings!

(When you've finished listening, hurry to page 14.)

If your answer was **A**, **YOU'RE CORRECT!** Mauna Kea, in Hawaii, rises over 10 200 metres from the bottom of the Pacific Ocean. That's over 1.4 kilometres taller than Mount Everest. Grab your passport. We're off to India.

Go to page 14

6 From Nepal to India

Days 32–40

Where is the worst weather in the world?

Some people say it's in the wettest place on Earth. Others may say the worst weather is in the coldest place on Earth. Others still will argue that the worst weather can be found in the hottest place on Earth.

In north-eastern India, where we're heading now, the village of Mawsynram is the *wettest* place on Earth. Every year, during the monsoon season, almost twelve metres of rain falls! That extreme weather causes flooding. But, while many people think this is terrible weather, the locals say it is good for crops and provides good supplies of water for people and animals.

In Al 'Aziziyah, Libya, temperatures as high as 57.8° Celsius have been recorded. That's hot! People from colder climates may say this is the worst weather in the world because it is too hot to do anything. But the locals here say that their clothing and lifestyle is suited to hot temperatures, and they are used to hot, sunny days.

People from both India and Libya would probably agree that the *coldest* place on Earth has the worst weather. But people who live in places where ice and snow are common would have a different view.

Everyone has a different opinion on where the worst weather is – but it is probably going to be the place that has the opposite weather to what people are used to.

children playing in a flooded street in India during the monsoon

Intrepid Travellers' Question

Where is the world's coldest place?

A. In your freezer, behind the ice-cream

B. In the Arctic

C. In the Antarctic

If your answer was **A** or **B**, here's **AN EXTREME CHALLENGE.** You can warm up on a beach at Christmas Island – but you'll have to share it with 120 million red crabs! From December to March, these crabs scramble from their burrows to the sea to lay their eggs.

(When you've finished warming up, hurry to page 16.)

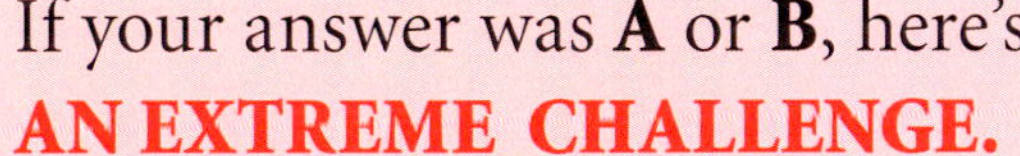

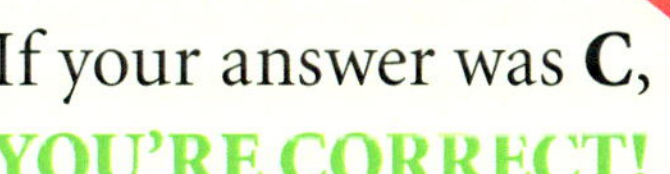

If your answer was **C**, **YOU'RE CORRECT!** The coldest place on Earth is in Antarctica, at Russia's Vostok Station. In 1983, the temperature was minus 89.2° Celsius! Grab your passport. We're off to the Maldives.

Go to page 16

7 From India to the Maldives

Days 41–47

India was nice, but it's time to dry out now. We are going to sail south-west to the Maldives. Don't bother looking for mountains or hills from the deck because the Maldives are flat. That makes people worried, as the effects of global warming may cause sea levels to rise over their islands.

After seven days in the Maldives, we'd better get to the airport before our feet get wet.

an island in the Maldives

Factopedia Fact

The Maldives is the lowest country on Earth. There are over 1100 islands in the Maldives. None of the islands is higher than 2.3 metres above sea level!

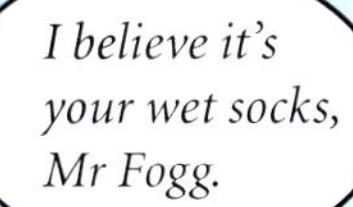

Fasten your seatbelts for a high-altitude landing!

Intrepid Travellers' Question

Where is the world's highest commercial airport?

A. In Nepal

B. In Hawaii

C. In China

If your answer was **A** or **B**, here's **AN EXTREME CHALLENGE.** Before you continue, you must go to the back of the queue at the world's busiest railway station. It's Shinjuku Station in Tokyo, Japan. Each day there will be 3.64 million people ahead of you!

(When you've finished queuing, hurry to page 18.)

If your answer was **C**, **YOU'RE CORRECT!** China's Qamdo Bangda Airport is 4334 metres above sea level. China also has the highest railway station and the highest road. Grab your passport. We're off to South Africa.

Go to page 18

From the Maldives to South Africa

Days 48–52

We're flying from the Maldives to South Africa, on our way to the deepest mine ever dug. It's the TauTona gold mine. It will take an hour to travel almost four kilometres below the surface. That far down, the air temperature is a very hot 55° Celsius!

While we're in Africa, we'll also visit the Nile River.

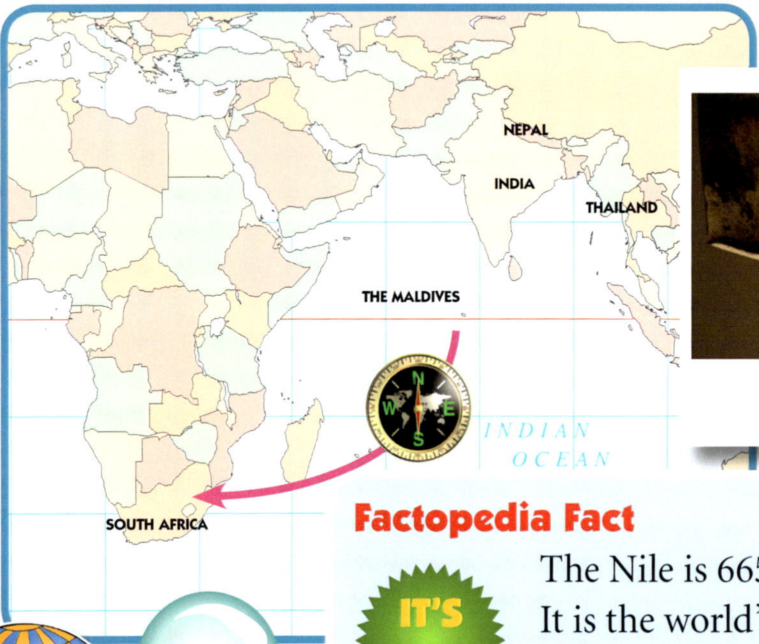

Gold mining is hot and dangerous work.

Factopedia Fact

IT'S TRUE!

The Nile is 6650 kilometres long. It is the world's longest river. But if we measure how much water spills from the river's mouth, it may not be the biggest in the world!

Oops, did we turn the taps off before we left, Mr Fogg?

sailing on the river Nile

Intrepid Travellers' Question

The Amazon is the world's biggest river. Where is it?

A. In Africa

B. In South America

C. In North America

If your answer was **A** or **C**, here's **AN EXTREME CHALLENGE.** Before you continue, you will be dropped into the world's deepest cave – 2191 metres deep. Voronya is in Georgia, a country on the Black Sea. I hope you brought extra batteries for your torch!

(When you've finished caving, hurry to page 20.)

If your answer was **B**, **YOU'RE CORRECT!** The Amazon River in South America is 6400 kilometres long. About 219 000 cubic metres of water travels past its mouth every second. Grab your passport. We're off to Bouvet Island.

Go to page 20

From South Africa to Bouvet Island

Days 53–62

If we head 2500 kilometres south-west from South Africa, we might spot Bouvet Island in the Atlantic Ocean. It is the most remote place in the world. It is furthest from land or people. The nearest land is 1600 kilometres to the south – an uninhabited part of Antarctica.

But we're going north – if you solve the next challenge correctly.

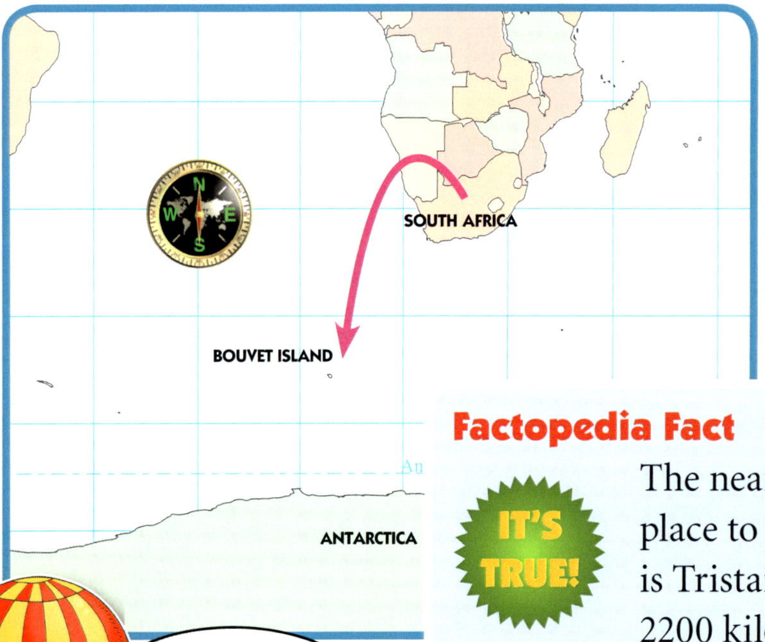

Bouvet Island

Factopedia Fact

IT'S TRUE!

The nearest inhabited place to Bouvet Island is Tristan da Cunha, 2200 kilometres away. Tristan da Cunha is the most remote inhabited group of islands in the world.

It looks lonely down there, Passepartout!

old wooden houses in the Norwegian countryside

Intrepid Travellers' Question

Bouvet Island is a Norwegian territory. Norway also has which of these:

A. **A town with the shortest name**

B. **The most northerly coral reef**

C. **The most northerly cinema and swimming pool**

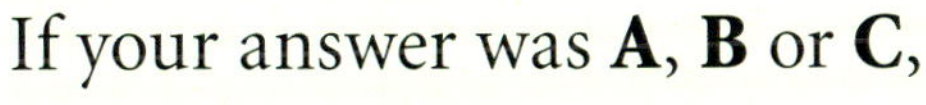

If your answer was **A**, **B** or **C**,

YOU'RE CORRECT!

Norway has a town with the shortest name – Å. There's a coral reef off the northern coast of Norway, and a cinema and swimming pool in Svalbard, in the Arctic Ocean north of Norway and east of Greenland. Grab your passport. We're off to Alert!

Go to page 22

10 From Bouvet Island to Alert

Days 63–71

We're travelling to the most northerly inhabited town in the world. Alert is in Nunavut, Canada, just 817 kilometres from the North Pole. Only five people live there full time.

Intrepid Travellers' Question

Alert doesn't suffer from overcrowding, but the world's most densely populated place does. Where is it?

A. Macau

B. Beijing

C. Mumbai

a Macau street

If your answer was **B** or **C**, here's **AN EXTREME CHALLENGE.** You must find your friends in the world's largest shopping mall in Kuala Lumpur, Malaysia. It covers 700 000 square metres!

(When you've finished searching, hurry to page 23.)

If your answer was **A**, **YOU'RE CORRECT!** Macau is the most densely populated place in the world. Grab your passport. We're off to Antarctica.

Go to page 23

11 From Alert to Antarctica

Days 72–80

The final stop on our trip around the world is a long way south. We're heading down to Antarctica.

Antarctica is the coldest, driest and windiest place on Earth.

penguins in Antarctica

Factopedia Fact

The windiest place in Antarctica is Commonwealth Bay. There, winds can blow at up to 240 kilometres an hour.

Travel Back to the Start

We've been travelling for eighty days in the world's most extreme places. Now we're going back to warm Samoa. You can complete your trip around the world if you answer one more question.

back to sunny Samoa

Your FINAL Intrepid Travellers' Question

Why is it important to understand the extremes of our planet?

What's your answer? Discuss it with your friends and report back. But remember – the plane's leaving for Samoa in just a few moments, so hurry!

FINISH

Index

Glossary

commercial	A place that is used regularly and open to the public or businesses
cubic metres	A measure of volume, where something is one metre tall, one metre long and one metre deep
densely populated	A large number of people living in a limited space (such as a building, town or country)
intrepid	Fearless and adventurous
monsoon	A seasonal period of very high rainfall that usually occurs close to the equator
Norwegian territory	A piece of land that is owned and managed by the government of Norway
river mouth	The downstream end of a river, where it flows into the sea or a lake
uninhabited	A place where no humans live